by Amanda Litz

Illustrated by
Jamie Pogue

Traveler's Trunk Publishing
Cedar Springs, Michigan

To Jacob, Sierra, and Mason - you are my inspiration. Also, to Robin and Brent two of the best friends a person could have.
-A.L.

ISBN 978-0-9841496-0-5

www.travelerstrunkpublishing.com

Printed in the United States of America

CHAPTERS

CHAPTER 1
Grandma Addy

"Are we there yet?" Jacob asked for the fifth time since the trip started.

"Yeah, Dad, this trip takes forever," Sierra added.

"Yes, we're finally here," Dad replied, slowing the car as they rounded the last corner.

The kids craned their necks to see Great-Grandma Addy's big beautiful house come into view. It was an old Victorian manor with a fancy white porch that wrapped all the way around the house and matching white shutters on all the windows.

The moment the car stopped, Jacob unbuckled his seatbelt and bolted out, nearly tripping on his laces in his rush to escape.

"That sure was a long drive," he groaned as he bent to tie his shoes.

Sierra was a year and a half younger than her brother and about a half-second behind him. She raced out of the car and slammed the door shut. She didn't mind car trips, but she was in a hurry to find Brent. Sierra ran past Jacob, messing up his hair as she went.

"Hey, quit it," Jacob said angrily. Then he stood up and shook his fist at her. "I'll get you, Sierra!"

Sierra giggled and ran over to Mom for protection. She peered out around

Mom's very pregnant belly and flashed him a sassy smile, or at least it was meant to be. Her two front teeth were missing and that made her smile more funny than sassy.

Jacob laughed and smoothed down his sandy brown hair.

"All right you two, knock it off," Mom said, moving Sierra out of her way.

Sierra looked up at Mom, her blue-gray eyes sparkling with delight. "Is Brent here yet?"

3

Mom raised an eyebrow. "What kind of mischief are you guys planning today?"

Jacob and Sierra just smiled, then Sierra tugged on Jacob's shirt. "Let's go find Brent."

The two of them raced into the house, leaving Mom and Dad behind.

Brent was seven years old and had been best friends with Jacob and Sierra since they were babies. They played together all the time until he had to move to Virginia with Aunt Robin. Now they only see each other at the family reunions in Michigan.

Jacob and Sierra found Brent sitting at the kitchen table playing with a monster truck all by himself. Most of the other children in the house were much older than him. They were in junior high and too old to play with a seven year old, except for Maggie. She was just a baby and too busy chewing on a plastic Pooh toy to notice him.

Brent's back was to the door as they walked into the room. Sierra had a great idea.

"Shhh," She said as she tapped Jacob on the shoulder and nodded toward Brent. Jacob knew what Sierra was thinking and nodded his head in agreement. They got down on their hands and knees and quietly crawled behind his chair. Then they both jumped up at the same time, yelling, "Boo!"

Brent jumped so high that he knocked the chair over backwards and tumbled out of it.

"Hey!" Brent shouted, his brown eyes twinkling with laughter. "I thought you guys would never get here. I've been waiting for hours."

Actually, it had only been about twenty minutes since he got there, but when you're seven, that can seem like a very long time.

"Have you seen Grandma Addy yet?" Jacob asked Brent.

"No, have you?" Brent stood up and rubbed the back of his head.

"We just got here," Sierra said, smoothing the wrinkles out of her new blue dress.

Jacob suddenly turned and ran out of the kitchen, shouting, "Let's go find Grandma Addy!"

Brent looked at Sierra. She shrugged and they both went running after him.

The kids loved to visit with Grandma Addy. She had a soft voice that made them feel warm and cozy, like fuzzy slippers, and she smelled like peppermint.

Whenever the kids would visit, she would tell them fantastic stories about far-off places. They were all adventures she claimed to have had when she was a little girl. Every story began in the attic with a trunk full of old clothes.

Jacob, Sierra, and Brent ran through the parlor, living room, and dining room before they found Grandma Addy in the sunroom.

"Grandma Addy! Grandma Addy! We missed you so much, tell us a story!"

She turned and smiled at them. "All right, all right, calm down," she said in her soft voice. "Would any of you children like a piece of candy? You may have one for each hand."

"That means two," Jacob replied.

"We know!" Sierra and Brent responded at the same time.

They each took their two pieces of candy and settled down on the floor by Grandma Addy's feet, ready to hear a story.

Grandma Addy must have talked for at least an hour, but they didn't even

notice the time going by. She told a tale of a great naval battle between the Queen's Guard, a magnificent battleship, and the Dark Marauder, a scary pirate ship. She described the naval officers she helped and the pirates she fought. Grandma Addy told the story so well that the three of them could picture it in their heads.

". . . and then I grabbed the rope and swung onto the pirate ship. I could see Admiral Gates and Captain Redbeard dueling on the top deck. I ran up the ladder to see if I could help. Just as I got there, Captain Redbeard knocked the sword out of the Admiral's hand.

It was all over. The pirates had won, unless I could save the Admiral. I quickly looked around. That's when I saw it, a cannonball rolling around on deck. I picked it up and put my best spin on it. I loved to bowl when I was a little girl and I was good, too. I aimed, took a few steps, and let the ball go. I watched it cross the deck. It seemed to go in slow motion.

Captain Redbeard had backed the Admiral against the rail. He was going to make him walk the plank. Just then, the cannonball reached the Captain. He was so surprised, it knocked his feet right out from under him. He dropped his sword and the Admiral grabbed it. And that's how I helped the Queen's Guard win the battle."

"That was a great story," Sierra said, looking at Grandma Addy in awe.

"Yeah, I wish I could fight pirates," Jacob added, jumping up and pretending to duel.

"How could a little kid really save the day?" Brent asked doubtfully.

"Oh, darling, you'd be surprised what a child can do, given the chance," she replied, smiling sweetly. "I'm tired now. Why don't you children go play for awhile? I'll see you before you leave." Grandma Addy gave them each a hug and sent them off to play.

Jacob, Sierra, and Brent headed for the backyard to play outside. Unfortunately, it began to rain. So, they had to stay in.

While they were exploring the upstairs rooms looking for something fun to do, the kids came across an old, frayed rope hanging down from the ceiling. It was at the end of a hallway and attached to what appeared to be a long trap door.

Jacob examined the rope. "This is very strange."

"I've never seen it here before, have you?" Brent looked at Jacob and Sierra quizzically.

Sierra shook her head. "Where do you think it came from?"

CHAPTER 2
The Attic

Jacob stretched up on his tiptoes and pulled the rope as hard as he could. The trap door flew open, covering them in dust. They had to quickly jump out of the way because a ladder dropped down right where they were standing. There was a loud thud as it hit the floor. Jacob, Sierra, and Brent looked up at the opening. It was as dark as a black hole in there.

"Go on, go check it out," Jacob said, pushing his sister toward the ladder.

"No way!" She backed up, looking at Brent.

"I don't think so," he said, crossing his arms over his chest.

"I dare you," Jacob said to his sister.

She shook her head.

"I double dare you," he added, satisfaction gleaming in his blue-green eyes. Sierra could never pass up a 'double dare.'

"Fine, if you two boys are chicken, then I'll do it," she replied. Sierra put her foot on the first step, took a deep breath, and began to climb.

There was an eerie silence as she made her way up the ladder. Sierra's palms began to sweat making it hard to hold on. The darkness was getting closer. One more step and she'd be there.

"I can't chicken out," she thought.

Sierra slowly peeked up into the attic. It was so dark, like entering another world. She couldn't see a thing, so she ran her hands across the attic floor. Sierra felt something hard under her hand. It was a flashlight. She picked it up and turned it on, then disappeared into the attic.

It was dusty and there were cobwebs in the corners, but it wasn't scary. Sierra looked around for a light switch. She saw a pull string and gave it a tug. With a quick glance, she noticed boxes stacked along the walls and a tall mirror off to one side. Next to the mirror there was a large trunk. It looked old and had a big lock on it.

Sierra turned around to call to the boys and bumped right into Jacob. She screamed, he stumbled back into Brent, and they all landed in heap on the floor.

"You scared me!" Sierra pushed her brother off of her.

"It's not my fault," Jacob responded, rolling off of Brent.

Brent's only reply was to rub his elbow and glare at both of them.

Then they all stood up and began to look around curiously. The attic was packed full of boxes, old toys, and other things nobody used anymore.

Sierra touched an old spinning wheel. "I saw one of these in Sleeping Beauty," she said. "It must be two hundred years old."

Jacob saw an old tub and washboard. He ran his hand down the washboard. "Could you imagine washing your clothes with this," he said. "I thought we had it rough when Mom asks us to put the clothes in the washer."

Brent picked up a large wooden spoon and poked at a fly caught in a spider web. "Do you think this is the attic from all of Grandma Addy's stories?"

"Well, she was born in this house like, a hundred years ago," Jacob replied, blowing dust off an old train set.

"If this is the attic, then this could be the trunk." Sierra pointed at the old trunk by the mirror in the corner.

The trunk was covered in brown leather with tarnished brass fittings on the corners. It had a lot of scratches from heavy use and was very dirty with age. It was shaped like a rectangle and about the size of a coffee table. The lid of the trunk was rounded and it had two straps with buckles, one on each side. Between the two buckles there was a large brass lock.

Jacob walked over and tried to open it. "I think it's locked."

"Then let's find the key." Sierra turned to look in the boxes behind her and began to laugh. Brent was buried waist-deep in a box, his legs waving around in the air.

"What are you doing?" she asked.

"Duh, I'm looking for the key!" Brent kicked his legs one more time and the whole box tipped over, spilling him onto the floor. "It's not in there," he said with a sheepish grin.

Jacob and Sierra joined the search. They looked in every box they could find. They looked in all the nooks and crannies and every corner of the room.

"Where could it be?" Brent asked.

"I don't know. We've looked everywhere." Jacob put down the jewelry box he was searching through and walked over to Brent and Sierra.

"It's not here!" Sierra stomped her foot. The floorboard under her came up, hitting Jacob right on the knee.

"OUCH!" he yelled, grabbing his leg and falling to the floor.

Brent bent over Jacob and looked in the hole where the floorboard used to be. It was dark, but he could see something down there. "Hand me the flashlight."

Sierra got the flashlight and shined the light in the hole.

"Hey, look at this!" Brent saw a big, old, rusty key. He reached in and pulled it out. It was covered in dust. Brent wiped the key on his shirt, smearing the dust all over his sleeve.

Sierra's eyes lit up with excitement. "Do you think this is it?"

"There's only one way to find out." Jacob grabbed the key from Brent. He rushed over to the trunk and jabbed it in.

The lock popped and the lid opened a little bit. Sierra was so excited she flipped the lid back. Its hinges creaked loudly, but it opened all the way.

CHAPTER 3
Imagination

Jacob, Sierra, and Brent leaned over the trunk. It was just as Grandma Addy had described it.

"They're so beautiful!" Sierra touched a pink dress made of silk. "Look at all these dresses. There must be one in every color!"

She picked up a green dress made of wool and found more things hidden under it. "Wow, there are matching hats and gloves for all the dresses, too. I'm in Heaven."

"Who cares about the dresses," Brent said, picking up some suspenders.

"What are these?" He stretched them a couple times and then tossed them over his shoulder.

"There sure are a lot of pants and shirts in here." Brent picked up a black suit coat. "Some poor guy is probably really cold right now with all his clothes packed away."

"These clothes look at least a hundred years old, so he's probably dead by now," Jacob stated plainly.

"Yeah, from the cold," Brent chuckled.

"Wow, look at this!" Jacob picked up a polished wooden cane with a silver head shaped like a dragon. Its emerald eyes flashed green in the dim attic light. Then he picked up several more canes, each with a different silver head on it. "I bet the man who owned these was very important, a doctor or a lawyer maybe."

The three of them pulled out clothes, canes, hats, gloves, and jewelry. It was hard to believe that one trunk could hold so much.

Sierra grabbed a beautiful blue hat with peacock feathers in it and placed it on her head. It slid down over her eyes. She pushed it back up.

"Could you imagine being in one of Grandma Addy's stories? I'd be an Admiral's daughter in a pirate story. I'd be captured by pirates, waiting to walk the plank."

She slipped on a pair of soft white gloves followed by a long, beautiful blue

dress that matched the hat. The clothes were much too big, but Sierra didn't care. She was having too much fun pretending.

Jacob smiled. "Yeah, I would be a Captain on the Admiral's ship. I would fight off the pirates and rescue you." He put on a red jacket that looked a lot like an old British officer's coat. Then he picked two canes up off the floor and pretended they were swords.

Brent laughed at them. "It would be fun to be in one of her stories." He slipped on an old vest that hung down to his knees and covered his black hair with a stocking cap.

"I would be a stowaway," he said. "I would sneak onto the pirate ship at one of the ports and search for a treasure map. Then, I could help you save the Admiral's daughter and we could all find the treasure together."

They all closed their eyes and wished they could have a grand adventure like Grandma Addy used to have. When they opened their eyes, they couldn't believe what they saw.

CHAPTER 4
Arrrr These Pirates Real?

Sierra found herself staring into the black eyes of a very dirty looking pirate.

"What happened?" she gasped. She tried to stand up, but her hands were tied behind her back.

The beautiful blue dress fit her perfectly. Her dark blonde hair was all in curls, and the blue hat was perched neatly on her head.

"Arrrr, Peg-Leg, let's make her walk the plank," growled a pirate with a skull-and-crossbones tattoo on his forearm.

"Not yet, Bones, we have to wait for the Captain," said Peg-Leg, tapping his wooden leg on the deck.

A pirate with a patch over his left eye tugged on Sierra's dress. "We should ransom her. Look  at her fancy clothes. I bet she's worth a lot of money."

"Take your hands off the girl, One Eye," said Peg-Leg. "I *said* we have to wait for the Captain."

Sierra yanked her dress out of One Eye's hand and glared at him. She was surrounded by dirty, evil pirates and she didn't know what to do. So, Sierra did the only thing she could think of.

"AHHHH!" She screamed so loud, all the pirates jumped back, covering their ears. Peg-Leg was so startled that he fell overboard with a loud splash.

Jacob was alone in a small rowboat heading toward the pirate ship. He was dressed in a full captain's uniform. The shiny brass buttons of his red officer's coat gleamed in the sunlight.

"Where am I?" he wondered. "And where did I get these?" Jacob noticed two swords with silver hilts attached to his belt.

The gentle swooshing of the water was the only sound he could hear until the scream echoed across the ocean. He would know that shriek anywhere. That was his sister. He began to row as fast as he could toward the pirate ship. He had to save Sierra.

Brent peered out from his hiding spot under the Captain's bed. He pushed his stocking cap back away from his eyes. He could see them standing around a table with a map of islands on it.

"My gut tells me it's on Three Cove Island," the red-haired pirate said as he patted his belly.

"That's just lunch talking, Red. I bet it's this one," said the pirate with the parrot. "It's called Golden Sands Island. What do you think Smithy?"

Smithy grabbed the rolled up treasure map from the Captain's bed, tapping Polly Pete on the chest with it. "No, Polly Pete, it's this one. The gypsy I stole this treasure map from told me so."

The Captain pulled out a dagger and slammed it down on the table. It stuck in the middle of a small island to the west.

"The treasure is here," he growled.

The other men quickly nodded their heads in agreement. No one ever dared to argue with Captain Blackheart. Just looking at him scared most people. He dressed all in black, his long coat brushing the top of his shiny knee-high boots, and his black hair and beard hung down in a mass of tangles.

Without warning, a scream ripped through the cabin walls. Brent jumped, hitting his head on the bottom of the Captain's bed.

Smithy was so startled that he dropped the treasure map and forgot all about it. Captain Blackheart grabbed his dagger from the table, and all of the pirates quickly ran out of the room.

"This is my chance," Brent thought.

He crawled out from under the bed, glanced at the island the captain had marked, then snatched the treasure map from the floor. He carefully rolled it up, put it in a scroll case, and stuck it in his shirt.

Now he just had to find a way off the ship. He quietly opened the door to see if anyone was in the hallway. It was clear, so he slowly crept out of the room.

Jacob pulled the rowboat along side the pirate ship. He tied the boat to the anchor and climbed up the chain onto the ship.

"I must be careful or the pirates will see me," he thought.

Jacob slowly crawled across the deck, hiding behind barrels and masts as he went. He needed to get close enough to rescue his sister.

The pirates were all gathered around Sierra. Her body lay limp, as if she were sleeping on the deck. The captain glared down at her.

"Smithy, wake that girl up!" he shouted.

Smithy picked up a bucket of water. He was about to throw it on Sierra when she jumped up and kicked him in the shin. He grabbed his leg and howled in pain, dropping the bucket on One Eye's foot.

"OWW!" One Eye shouted, hopping around like a kangaroo, on one foot. He bumped into several other pirates and they all tumbled over.

Now was the time to escape. Sierra and Brent both ran toward the rowboats on the side of the ship, while Jacob jumped out from behind a barrel with two swords drawn and began to fight the pirates.

Sierra tried to lower a rowboat with her hands tied, but she couldn't. Brent saw the problem and untied her. Then they worked together to get the boat down.

Brent was stepping over the side of the ship when Smithy grabbed him by the vest. Sierra picked up a mop and knocked Smithy over the side, freeing Brent.

"Thanks," Brent said, turning over a barrel and rolling it at One Eye.

On the other side of the deck, Jacob fought pirates on all sides. First he clashed with Red, easily knocking the sword out of his hand and pushing him overboard. Then he turned to duel Peg-Leg. Jacob cracked his wooden leg, causing him to fall to the deck. Bones tried to tackle him, but Jacob jumped out of the way, and Bones fell down a hatch.

"Help! Help!"

Sierra's terrified shouts got Jacob's attention. He could see Brent and Sierra standing back to back at the end of a plank. Captain Blackheart, Polly Pete, and a very wet Smithy had captured them. Captain Blackheart was going to make them walk the plank.

Jacob had an idea. He dropped his swords and ran to the mast closest to the pirates. He quickly climbed up the mast and untied the rope connecting the sail to it. The sail fell on the pirates, trapping them under the heavy canvas.

"Phew, I thought we were going overboard for sure," Brent sighed.

"Let's get off this plank." Sierra grabbed Brent's hand and carefully walked back on the ship.

The pirates were struggling under the sail, pushing and pulling, trying to find their way out.

"I'll get you kids!" Captain Blackheart shouted as he stuck his dagger through the canvas and began to cut his way out of the sail.

"We have to go!" Sierra and Brent ran to the other side of the deck where the rowboat was tied. They quickly climbed down to the boat together.

"Wait for me," Jacob hollered as he dove from the mast into the ocean. Seconds later, his head popped up from the water and Jacob climbed into the boat, breathing a sigh of relief.

"Where do we go now?" Sierra looked around the vast open space. The ocean seemed to go on forever. There was no land in sight.

"How about a treasure hunt?" Brent suggested, pulling the scroll case from his shirt.

CHAPTER 5
Island Adventure

"A treasure hunt?" Jacob and Sierra looked at Brent in disbelief.

"How are we going to hunt for treasure? We're in a tiny boat." Jacob tapped his foot on the wooden boards. "There's nowhere to dig."

Brent pulled the treasure map out of the scroll case. "I stole this map from the pirates. I heard them talking about the treasure. The Captain said it's on an island to the west." Brent's brown eyes flashed with excitement.

"If you help me find the gold, I'll split it with you," he added.

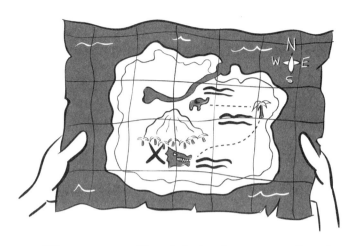

"Do you really think that map leads to a treasure? It sounds like fiction to me." Jacob was rowing the boat and looking around for an island close by, secretly hoping there was a treasure.

"I bet there's a wonderful treasure full of jewels and gold and diamond necklaces!" Sierra exclaimed. She smiled at the thought of herself wearing a crown sparkling with rubies, emeralds, and sapphires.

"I don't think the pirates would be after it if it wasn't there." Brent tried to convince them.

"All right then, let's find some treasure." Jacob and Sierra agreed.

Brent glanced around the seemingly endless ocean. "Which way is west?"

Jacob pulled a compass out of his jacket pocket and opened the lid. "That way!" he pointed.

"What's that?" Sierra leaned over to examine the compass.

"It's a compass. It shows you which direction is north and from that you can find east, south, and west." Jacob flipped the lid closed and put it back in his pocket. "Over there," he pointed. "I think that could be the island."

Brent and Sierra squinted at the dark lump in the distance. "I think you're right," they agreed.

Jacob began to row toward the island. Time seemed to pass very slowly and he was getting tired.

"I'm bored," Brent grumbled.

Jacob looked over at Brent. He was leanig back against the side of the boat balancing the scroll case on his nose.

"You could always take a turn rowing if you're really that bored," replied Jacob, offering Brent the oars.

Just then, a large wave rocked the boat and the scroll case went flying off Brent's nose into the ocean.

"Oh no!" Brent jumped into the water to get the map. The waves quickly carried the map and Brent farther and farther away from the boat.

Brent was a strong swimmer despite his small size. He caught up to the scroll case in no time.

"What's that behind Brent?" Sierra leaned over the side of the boat to get a better look.

Jacob put his hand above his eyes to block the sun. "It looks like a fin." He grabbed the oars and began to row. "We better get to him fast. It might be a …"

"It's a shark!" she screamed.

Sierra stood up and began yelling to Brent just as he grabbed the scroll case. "Brent, look out. Shark!"

Brent looked behind him. He saw the fin getting closer and closer. He turned and swam toward the boat as fast as he could.

Jacob yelled at Sierra. "Sit down before you fall in, too." He was rowing so hard his arms began to hurt.

They were almost there. Brent was reaching for the boat. Sierra leaned over the side to pull him in, but it was too late. The fin was right behind him.

Brent yelled, "Ahhhh! It bit me!"

Jacob and Sierra gasped in horror. Brent screamed in terror. It swam around the boat, poked its head out of the water and said, "EET, EET."

"That's not a shark," Jacob said. "It's a dolphin and I think he wants to play."

"Oh, he's so cute," Sierra said, reaching out to pat his head.

Brent looked at them bashfully. "I guess he just bumped me," he said with an impish grin.

Jacob and Sierra helped Brent into the boat and Brent rowed the rest of the way to the island so he wouldn't be bored.

The sun was high in the sky by the time they pulled the boat onto shore. They stood on a white sandy beach that lined the cove.

There was a tall mountain jutting up from the center of the island. It was so big, the top reached up into the clouds. The mountain was surrounded by a thick, lush, green jungle that stretched all the way to the beach.

Sierra saw bananas and coconuts high up in the trees. Her stomach growled. "I'm so hungry."

"Me too." Brent walked over to a coconut tree and began climbing it.

While Brent and Sierra were collecting fruit, Jacob did a little exploring and found a stream leading to the ocean. "This is a good place to get fresh water," he thought.

Jacob returned to get Brent and Sierra. "Hey guys, I found a place to get drinking water. Follow me." Jacob picked up some fruit and led the way.

"It's beautiful!" Sierra walked over to the stream to get a drink. "And delicious, too."

Brent sat down and picked up a coconut. "How do you open one of these?" He tried to crack it open by throwing it at a tree. It bounced off, nearly hitting Sierra. She just stuck her tongue out at him and peeled a banana.

Next, he tried a big rock. He held the coconut still and brought the rock down as hard as he could.

"Ow!" He hit his thumb instead.

"You will open, Coconut." He picked it up and hit the coconut with his head so hard he saw stars.

Jacob laughed and took the coconut from Brent. He wedged it between two

exposed roots and showed Brent how to use a heavy stick to pound a sharp rock into its husk. "I saw this on the Discovery Channel."

Brent was skeptical, but he did what Jacob said, and within minutes, he was drinking sweet coconut milk.

The kids ate all the fruit they had collected. Once their bellies were full, Brent unrolled the treasure map. It was time for the hunt to begin.

CHAPTER 6
Hunting for Treasure

The map was a sketch of the island, including the stream and the mountain they had seen. It had three large pictures on it: an elephant, a tree, and a dragon. The images were connected by a dotted line and there was a clue under each one. The X that marked the treasure was next to the dragon.

"If we're going to find the treasure, we need to solve these clues." Jacob ran his finger across the first clue, paying careful attention to each word.

The first clue was under the drawing of an elephant. It said:

Go to the place where the elephant sprays water over a rainbow.

"Do you think there are elephants on this island?" Sierra imagined a whole herd of elephants playing in a pool, spraying each other with water.

Brent thought about the elephants he had seen at the circus. "Do you think we can ride them?" he wondered.

"I don't think an elephant would stay in one place just waiting for someone to hunt for treasure. I think we should find something that looks like an elephant." Jacob scanned the horizon. "Now we just have to figure out where to start searching."

"Wherever the peanuts are," Brent chuckled.

"Maybe by some water," Sierra suggested, "since it's supposed to be spraying water."

"Good idea. Let's follow the stream." Jacob took the map from Brent, rolled it up, and headed upstream.

Sierra and Brent followed closely behind him as they entered the jungle.

Sierra looked around in wonder. "Have you ever seen anything so beautiful?" She stopped to watch hundreds of butterflies take flight, coloring the sky orange, yellow, and purple.

"Check that out." Jacob pointed to two crocodiles sunning themselves on a large rock. A third one poked its eyes out of the water and blinked.

Brent saw a black panther up in a tree. "Guys, maybe we should save the sightseeing for later." He nodded toward the panther.

Its bright green eyes seemed to glow as it watched them. The panther licked its lips and stretched.

"Maybe we ought to hurry up." Jacob quickened his steps along with Brent and Sierra.

The jungle opened up into a large clearing. The three of them saw a giant waterfall pouring down into a pool. The cliff was angled up and it sprayed the water out like a spout.

"Look!" Brent signaled to the waterfall. "It looks like an elephant spraying water."

"There's the rainbow!" Sierra shouted excitedly.

"This must be it. What's the next clue?" Jacob unrolled the map to read the second clue.

It said:

In the morning, you must walk one hundred and fifty paces from the elephant with the sun in your face. There you will find the lovers' trees.

"I don't want to wait until morning. Let's just go now." Brent pulled on Sierra impatiently.

Sierra motioned to the sun. "The sun is over there. We just need to walk toward it."

They both began to head into the sun counting their steps when Jacob shouted, "Stop!"

Brent and Sierra froze.

Jacob put his hand out. "You're going the wrong way."

"What do you mean we're going the wrong way?" Sierra argued. "The sun is over there."

"You're right, but it's almost night time. The sun comes up in the east and goes down in the west. So, we must go

away from the sun." Jacob nodded in satisfaction.

Sierra crossed her arms over her chest and raised her eyebrow. "How do you know?"

Jacob smiled. "I learned it in school."

Brent didn't want to wait for them to stop arguing. He decided to walk with his back to the sun, counting his steps as he went. "One, two, three ..."

Jacob and Sierra noticed Brent was gone. "Wait for us!" they shouted, running after him.

When they caught up to him, they heard him counting, "One hundred forty-eight, one hundred forty-nine, one hundred and fifty." Brent stopped. "This is it."

Jacob looked around doubtfully. "Where are the lovers' trees?"

"What do lovers' trees look like?" Brent scratched his head in wonder.

Jacob shrugged.

"There!" Sierra jumped up and down excitedly. "Those are lovers' trees." She pointed at two palm trees that grew out of the ground next to each other.

Their trunks bowed out away from each other, but at the top their leaves leaned back in toward each other. The two trees looked like a big heart.

"Good job." Jacob patted Sierra's shoulder. "What's the next clue?"

CHAPTER 7
On the Run

Just as Jacob asked the question, the kids heard a gunshot and loud voices.

Sierra glanced at the boys nervously. "Could the pirates have found us already?"

"Arrrr, we know you're here. We found your boat!" Bones bellowed through the trees.

"We want our treasure map back!" Captain Blackheart roared.

Brent climbed a tree to get a better look. He could see the pirates on the beach. "They're by the stream," he said, dropping down out of the tree.

"Maybe we should set a trap like in the movie Swiss Family Robinson," Sierra suggested.

"We don't have time." Jacob unrolled the map again. "We need to find that treasure."

The third clue said:

Go through the lovers' trees and walk seventy-five paces. Then turn right and walk another one hundred paces. There you will see the dragon's mouth. Enter, but beware of its fire.

Sierra's shoulders slumped. "I don't know what's worse, dragons or pirates."

"I hope the dragon isn't angry," squeaked Brent.

Jacob grabbed Brent and Sierra by the hand and pulled them through the lovers' trees. The kids quickly counted their paces. When they reached seventy-five, they stopped.

Jacob frowned, stroking his chin. "Which way do we turn?"

"I think it was left, no, right." Brent looked at Sierra for support.

Sierra nodded her head in agreement. "It was right. I'm sure of it."

Jacob, Sierra, and Brent promptly turned and counted to one hundred. As they finished counting, they came into a clearing at the bottom of a giant mountain.

Brent threw his hands up in the air. "What do we do now?"

"Over there." Jacob gestured to a large cave that stuck out from the base

of the mountain.

They approached slowly and looked inside. There were pointed rocks that came down from the ceiling and up from the floor of the cave.

Sierra shivered as she looked into the mouth of the cave. "They sure do look like teeth."

"Yeah, angry teeth!" Brent gulped.

"What was that?" Jacob turned around just in time to see the pirates crashing through the trees. "Those teeth don't look as angry as the pirates." He quickly pushed Sierra and Brent into the cave.

They ran a short distance, then slowed down. The deeper they went, the harder it was to see. The jagged cave walls were barely visible in the dim light.

Brent sniffed the air and wrinkled his nose. "What's that awful smell?"

Jacob took a deep breath. "I think it's sulfur. I have some in my chemistry set."

Sierra plugged her nose. "Other than the smell, it's not so bad."

"Not yet," replied Brent, "but we haven't seen its fire."

Jacob grabbed Brent and Sierra to stop them. "I think we just did." He pointed to a narrow river of lava straight ahead. "This isn't a mountain, it's a volcano."

CHAPTER 8
Dragon's Fire

"A volcano!" Brent and Sierra quickly stepped back, bumping into Jacob.

"We have to get out of here." Brent turned around to run.

Jacob held on to Brent's shirt. "No, the pirates will be here soon. We have to get across the lava."

Sierra tapped Jacob on the shoulder, then pointed. "Look up there. It's a bridge."

The boys looked up and saw a rope bridge about twenty feet above the lava. Sierra ran over to the wall where the bridge was attached.

"It looks like someone cut steps into the wall." She put her foot on the first step and slowly began to climb. Sierra's palms began to sweat and her hand slipped.

"Be careful!" Brent shouted up the steps. "You almost fell."

When she reached the top, Sierra carefully put her foot on the bridge to test it. "It's okay. Follow me."

The bridge creaked and swung as they added all their weight to it. Sierra was almost across when she heard a loud crack behind her.

She turned around just as Brent fell through the bridge. Jacob leaped forward and caught his hand. Sierra quickly ran back to help. Jacob was lying on the bridge, holding Brent with both hands.

Brent dangled above the lava, "Don't let me fall!"

Jacob pulled as hard as he could. He started to lift Brent onto the bridge.

Sierra grabbed Brent under the arms to help pull him up. Frantic, they hurried across before anyone else fell through.

Once they were back on the ground, they all breathed a sigh of relief.

"That was scary!" Brent dropped to his knees and kissed the ground.

Sierra looked around the cave. "What now?"

Jacob unrolled the map. "We look for the X that marks the spot."

Sierra found two planks nearby, one crossed over the other. "Over here, this must be it!"

Brent jumped up. "Let's start digging!"

They all ran over to the spot. Jacob tossed the boards aside. The three of them began to dig in the sandy floor with their hands. They dug down about a foot and hit something hard.

"We found it!" they shouted and began to dig faster.

The kids dug all around it until they could reach in and pull it up. It was very heavy; all three of them had to pull it out of the ground. Jacob tried to open it, but it was locked.

Brent kicked the chest and moaned. "We don't have a key."

Jacob thought for a moment. "I know what to do." He pulled a hat pin out of Sierra's hat. "Remember how Grandma Addy escaped from the tower in her story about the evil king?"

"Ahha," Sierra handed Jacob a rock.

He put the hat pin into the keyhole and tapped it twice with the rock. The lock was old and rusty, so it popped open with little effort.

Sierra was so excited, she swung the lid right open. They all stared in amazement.

"Whoa!" Brent dipped his hands into the treasure chest, scooping up gold doubloons, diamonds, rubies, and emeralds.

"I wonder who this belonged to." Jacob grabbed a heavy gold crown with a single blue stone.

Sierra picked out a diamond necklace and held it up. "Isn't it beautiful?"

Just then, Captain Blackheart and his crew appeared on the other side of the lava.

"Hey, Me Hardies, they've found our treasure," he growled. "Get them!"

Brent dropped the gold coins he was holding. "What are we going to do?"

Jacob looked for an escape route. "We're trapped."

The pirates were crossing the rope bridge. Sierra closed her eyes and whispered, "I wish we could go home."

Brent and Jacob looked at each other, trembling with fear. They closed their eyes too and whispered over and over, "I wish we could go home."

CHAPTER 9
Safe Return

When they opened their eyes, they noticed there were no pirates, no lava, and no treasure. They were safe. Jacob, Sierra, and Brent were standing in the attic, still wearing the dress-up clothes from the trunk.

"Had it all been a dream?" Jacob looked around the attic in wonder.

Brent shook his head in disbelief. "It couldn't have been real, could it?"

Jacob turned to Sierra and Brent. "Did you see the pirates?"

Brent cleared his throat. "Did you see the treasure?"

They all nodded their heads in amazement. Sierra looked down and noticed she was still holding a beautiful diamond necklace in her hands.

"Look," she whispered to the boys.

Jacob and Brent stared at the necklace in her hands. Had she found it in the traveler's trunk or was it really from the treasure chest?

"Jacob, Sierra, it's time to go home!"

Jacob looked toward the attic entrance. "That sounds like Mom."

"Brent, where are you?"

"Mine, too," Brent added.

"Yeah, we better get down there." Sierra placed the necklace in the trunk.

The kids quickly put everything back. Jacob locked the trunk, and Brent put the key under the floorboard to keep it safe. Taking one last look at the trunk, they all headed down the steps.

Jacob closed the trap door, looking around to make sure no one saw them. "Let's go find Grandma Addy."

Jacob, Sierra, and Brent ran through the parlor, living room and dining room looking for Grandma Addy. They finally found her still sitting in the sunroom.

The three of them were so excited they were all talking at once.

"Grandma Addy, are the stories all true?"

"We were in the attic!"

"We found the old trunk!"

"Something amazing happened!"

"There were pirates!"

"We had a grand adventure just like you!"

Grandma Addy slowly turned in her wheelchair. "Calm down, children. I can only listen to one of you at a time." She gently placed her hand on Sierra's cheek. "I thought the attic was closed off, dear," she added with a wink.

Sierra wanted to tell her everything that had happened. She was so thrilled

to finally have a story to tell her, one that was just as exciting as any Grandma Addy had ever told.

Grandma Addy put a finger to her lips. "Your mother is looking for you and Jacob, so you can tell me all about your adventure the next time you come to visit."

Just then, Mom and Aunt Robin entered the room. "There you are." Mom put her hands on her hips. "Where have you been?"

"We've been looking all over for you guys," Aunt Robin added. "It's time to go. Say goodbye to Grandma Addy."

"Goodbye, Grandma Addy," they all said, giving her a big hug at the same time. "We love you!"

She hugged them back. "I love you, too, my sweet grandchildren, and I will see you soon."

Jacob, Sierra, and Brent waved goodbye as they left. They couldn't wait to come back for another grand adventure with the traveler's trunk.

Dear Reader,

Since I was a little girl, I have been telling stories about imaginary adventures to anyone who would listen. When I became a mother, I began telling these stories to my children.

One night while I was putting Jacob and Sierra to bed, along with my college roommate's son Brent, they asked me to make-up a story about them. I thought for a moment about all the different games they played. The kids loved to dress up and pretend to be superheroes, or knights and princesses. I imagined how fun it would be if they could have a real adventure and that's when I came up with the idea of a magic traveler's trunk.

I know that kids can tell amazing stories, too. That's why I'll be publishing one kid's story a month on the Traveler's Trunk Publishing website at www.travelerstrunkpublishing.com. So, sit down, grab a pen and paper, and write an adventure that you would like to have with the Traveler's Trunk. I can't wait to read it!

Send your story along with Permission Slip to:
Traveler's Trunk Publishing
c/o Amanda Litz
15071 Hanna Ave NE
Cedar Springs, MI 49319

I hope you enjoyed reading Pirate's Treasure and will come back to see what new adventures Jacob, Sierra, and Brent will have with the Traveler's Trunk next.

Permission Slip

**For a chance to have your story published
on the Traveler's Trunk Publishing website,
have your parents fill out this form.**

I, (parent's name) _____

give my permission to Amanda Litz, author of the

Traveler's Trunk Series and owner of Traveler's

Trunk Publishing, to publish my son/daughter's

(child's name) _____ story on her

website at www.travelerstrunkpublishing.com

_____

(Parent Signature)

_____

(Date)

**Please fill out preferred contact information
for notification:**

Phone: _____
Address: _____
_____
_____
Email: _____

Traveler's Trunk
Adventure Story

Write your own traveler's trunk story
by filling in the blanks in the following
pages. Read the description under each
blank to find out what kind of word to
use. Make sure you fill in all the
blanks before you read the story.

REMINDER

Noun: person, place, or thing

Verb: an action

Adjective: describes a noun

Last _____, I went on vaction with my
<small>time of year</small>

family to _____. My parents wanted
a state

to see the _____ _____, but I just
adjective   noun

wanted to go to _____ to see a _____.
a place   noun

On the way to _____ our car
same state

broke down and we had to stay at a

_____, old _____. While the car was
adjective   type of building

being _____, I decided to go exploring.
verb ending in -ed

I ran around the back of the _____
Same type of building

and _____ right into a _____ about
verb ending in -ed   something living

my age. I asked their name and they said

_____. _____ seemed like a nice
name   same name

_____, so I asked them to play with me.
same living thing

We walked through the woods for a

_____ before we saw it. It was a
short time span

creepy _____ with all the _____s
another type of building   noun

boarded up and no _____. There didn't
noun

seem to be anyone around so we went in.

We walked into a _____ room with
adjective

nothing in it, except an old trunk on the

_____. _____ and I were curious, so
indoor object   same name

we opened the trunk and saw a _____,
object 1

_____, & _____. _____ picked up
object 2   object 3   same name

a _____and put it on his/her _____.
same object 1   body part

_____ said, "I'm the great _____!"
same name   silly name

I laughed, picking up a _____ and
same object 3

using it as a _____. "I'm _____,
noun   another silly name

ruler of all the land."

The next thing we knew, we were

_____s standing at the _____.
what you dream of being   place you want to be

There was a _____ in front of us and
                    group of people

a _____ behind us.
same group of people

"This can't be happening," I said.

_____ just _____ and ran down to
same name   verb ending in -ed

join them. I didn't know what else to do,

so I _____, and then ran after them.
   verb ending in -ed

We _____ all afternoon, and then it
something you want to do (past tense)

was done. We had won.

I was getting _____ and wished we
adjective

could go home. _____ agreed, and then
same name

mysteriously we were back, holding

the _____ and _____.
same object 1   same object 3

I never saw _____ again after that,
same name

but I bet he still remembers our _____
adjective

adventure with the trunk.